STUBBY PRINGLE'S CHRISTMAS

Also by Jack Schaefer

The Big Range
The Canyon
Company of Cowards
First Blood and Other Stories
Heroes without Glory
The Kean Land and Other Stories
Mavericks
Monte Walsh
Old Ramon
The Pioneers
Shane

STUBBY PRINGLE'S CHRISTMAS

JACK SCHAEFER

ILLUSTRATIONS BY
LORENCE BJORKLUND

University of New Mexico Press | Albuquerque

University of New Mexico Press edition published 2017
by arrangement with the Jack Schaefer Trust
Printed in the United States of America

22 21 20 19 18 17   1 2 3 4 5 6

Library of Congress Cataloging-in-Publication Data is available online.

Cover illustrations by Lorence Bjorklund
Designed by Lila Sanchez
Composed in Adobe Jenson Pro 13/18. Display type is Adorn Copperplate.

FOR ALL MY GRANDCHILDREN THAT ARE
AND SHALL BE

HIGH ON THE MOUNTAINSIDE by the little line cabin in the crisp clean dusk of evening Stubby Pringle swings into saddle. He has shape of bear in the dimness, bundled thick against cold. Double socks crowd scarred boots. Leather chaps with hair out cover patched corduroy pants. Fleece-lined jacket with wear of winters on it bulges body and heavy gloves blunt fingers. Two gay red bandannas folded together fatten throat under chin. Battered hat is pulled down to sit on ears and in side pocket of jacket are rabbit-skin earmuffs he can put to use if he needs them.

Stubby Pringle swings up into saddle. He looks out and down over worlds of snow and ice and tree and rock. He spreads arms wide and they embrace whole ranges of hills. He stretches tall and hat brushes stars in sky. He is Stubby Pringle, cowhand of the Triple X, and this is his night to howl. He is Stubby Pringle, son of the wild jackass, and he is heading for the Christmas dance at the schoolhouse in the valley.

Stubby Pringle swings up and his horse stands like rock. This is the pride of his string, flop-eared ewe-necked cat-hipped strawberry roan that looks like it should have died weeks ago but has iron rods for bones and nitroglycerin for blood and can go from here to doomsday with nothing more than mouthfuls of snow for water and tufts of winter-cured bunch-grass snatched between drifts for food. It stands like rock. It knows the folly of trying to unseat Stubby. It wastes no energy in futile explosions. It knows that twenty-seven miles of hard winter going are foreordained for this evening and twenty-seven more of harder uphill return by morning. It has done this before. It is saving the dynamite under its hide for the destiny of a true cowpony which is to take its rider where he wants to go—and bring him back again.

Stubby Pringle sits in his saddle and he grins into cold and distance and future full of festivity. Join me in a look at what can be seen of him despite the bundling and frosty breath vapor that soon will hang icicles on his nose. Those are careless haphazard scrambled features under the low hat brim, about as handsome as a blue boar's snout. Not much fuzz yet on his chin. Why, shucks, is he just a boy? Don't make that mistake, though his twentieth birthday is still six weeks away. Don't make the mistake Hutch Handley made

last summer when he thought this was young unseasoned stuff and took to ragging Stubby and wound up with ears pinned back and upper lip split and nose mashed flat and the whole of him dumped in a rain barrel. Stubby has been taking care of himself since he was orphaned at thirteen. Stubby has been doing man's work since he was fifteen. Do you think Hardrock Harper of the Triple X would have anything but an all-around hard-proved hand up here at his farthest winter line camp siding Old Jake Hanlon, toughest hard-bitten old cowman ever to ride range?

Stubby Pringle slips gloved hand under rump to wipe frost off the saddle. No sense letting it melt into patches of corduroy pants. He slaps right-side saddle-bag. It contains a burlap bag wrapped around a two-pound box of candy, of fancy chocolates with variegated

interiors he acquired two months ago and has kept hidden from Old Jake. He slaps left-side saddlebag. It holds a burlap bag wrapped around a paper parcel that contains a close-folded piece of fine dress goods and a roll of pink ribbon. Interesting items, yes. They are ammunition for the campaign he has in mind to soften the affections of whichever female of right vintage among those at the schoolhouse appeals to him most and seems most susceptible.

Stubby Pringle settles himself firmly into the saddle. He is just another of far-scattered poorly-paid patched-clothes cowhands that inhabit these parts and likely marks and smells of his calling have not all been scrubbed away. He knows that. But this is his night to howl. He is Stubby Pringle, true-begotten son of the wildest jackass, and he has been riding line through hell and high water and winter storms for two months without a break and he has done his share of the work

and more than his share because Old Jake is getting along and slowing some and this is his night to stomp floorboards till schoolhouse shakes and kick heels up to lanterns above and whirl a willing female till she is dizzy enough to see past patched clothes to the man inside them. He wriggles toes deep into stirrups and settles himself firmly in the saddle.

"I could of et them choc'lates," says Old Jake from cabin doorway. "They wasn't hid good," he says. "No good at all."

"An' be beat like a drum," says Stubby. "An' wrung out like a dirty dishrag."

"By who?" says Old Jake. "By a young un like you? Why, I'd of tied you in knots afore you knew what's what iffen you tried it. You're a dang-blatted young fool," he says. "A ding-busted dang-blatted fool. Riding out on a night like this iffen it is Chris'mas eve. A dong-bonging ding-busted dang-blatted fool," he says. "But iffen I was your age agin, I reckon I'd be doing it too." He cackles like an old rooster. "Squeeze one of 'em for me," he says, and he steps back inside and he closes the door.

Stubby Pringle is alone out there in the darkening dusk, alone with flop-eared ewe-necked cat-hipped roan that can go to the last trumpet call under him and with cold of wicked winter wind around him and with twenty-seven miles of snow-dumped distance ahead of him. "Wahoo!" he yells. "Skip to my Lou!" he shouts. "Do-si-do and round about!"

He lifts reins and roan sighs and lifts feet. At easy warming-up amble they drop over the edge of benchland where cabin snugs into tall pines and on down great bleak expanse of mountainside.

STUBBY PRINGLE, SPURS AJINGLE, jogs upslope through crusted snow. The roan, warmed through, moves strong and steady under him. Line cabin and line work are far forgotten things back and back and up and up the mighty mass of mountain. He is Stubby Pringle, rooting tooting hard-working hard-playing cowhand of the Triple X, heading for the Christmas dance at the schoolhouse in the valley.

He tops out on one of the lower ridges. He pulls reins to give the roan a breather. He brushes icicles off his nose. He leans forward and reaches to brush several

more off sidebars of old bit in the bridle. He straightens
tall. Far ahead, over top of last and lowest ridge, on into
the valley, he can see tiny specks of glowing allure that
are schoolhouse windows. Light and gaiety and good
liquor and fluttering skirts are there. "Wahoo!" he yells.
"Gals an' women an' grandmothers!" he shouts. "Raise
your skirts and start askipping! I'm acoming!"

He slaps spurs to roan. It leaps like mountain lion, out and down, full into hard gallop downslope, rushing, reckless of crusted drifts and ice-coated bush-branches slapping at them. He is Stubby Pringle, born with spurs on, nursed on tarantula juice, weaned on rawhide, at home in the saddle of a hurricane in shape of horse that can race to outer edge of eternity and back, heading now for high jinks two months overdue. He is ten feet tall and the horse is gigantic, with wings, iron-boned and dynamite-fueled, soaring in forty-foot leaps down the flank of the whitened wonder of a winter world.

They slow at the bottom. They stop. They look up
the rise of the last low ridge ahead. The roan paws frozen ground and snorts twin plumes of frosty vapor.
Stubby reaches around to pull down fleece-lined jacket
that has worked a bit up back. He pats right-side
saddlebag. He pats left-side saddlebag. He lifts reins to
soar up and over last low ridge.

Hold it, Stubby. What is that? Off to the right.

He listens. He has ears that can catch snitch of
mouse chewing on chunk of bacon rind beyond the log
wall by his bunk. He hears. Sound of ax striking wood.

What kind of dong-bonging ding-busted dang-blatted fool would be chopping wood on a night like this and on Christmas Eve and with a dance underway at the schoolhouse in the valley? What kind of chopping is this anyway? Uneven in rhythm, feeble in stroke. Trust Stubby Pringle, who has chopped wood enough for cookstove and fireplace to fill a long freight train, to know how an ax should be handled.

There. That does it. That whopping sound can only mean that the blade has hit at an angle and bounced away without biting. Some dong-bonging ding-busted dang-blatted fool is going to be cutting off some of his own toes.

He pulls the roan around to the right. He is Stubby Pringle, born to tune of bawling bulls and blatting calves, branded at birth, cowman raised and cowman to the marrow, and no true cowman rides on without stopping to check anything strange on range. Roan chomps on bit, annoyed at interruption. It remembers who is in saddle. It sighs and obeys. They move quietly in dark of night past boles of trees jet black against dim greyness of crusted snow on ground. Light shows faintly ahead. Lantern light through a small oiled-paper window.

Yes. Of course. Just where it has been for eight
months now. The Henderson place. Man and woman
and small girl and waist-high boy. Homesteaders. Not
even fools, homesteaders. Worse than that. Out of their
minds altogether. All of them. Out here anyway. Betting
the government they can stave off starving for five years
in exchange for one hundred sixty acres of land. Land
that just might be able to support seven jack-rabbits
and two coyotes and nine rattlesnakes and maybe all of
four thin steers to a whole section. In a good year.

Homesteaders. Always out of almost everything, money and food and tools and smiles and joy of living. Everything. Except maybe hope and stubborn endurance.

Stubby Pringle nudges the reluctant roan along. In patch-light from the window by a tangled pile of dead tree branches he sees a woman. Her face is grey and pinched and tired. An old stocking cap is pulled down on her head. Ragged man's jacket bumps over long woolsey dress and clogs arms as she tries to swing an ax into a good-sized branch on the ground.

Whopping sound and ax bounces and barely misses an ankle.

"Quit that!" says Stubby, sharp. He swings the roan in close. He looks down at her. She drops ax and backs away, frightened. She is ready to bolt into two-room bark-slab shack. She looks up. She sees that haphazard scrambled features under low hat brim are crinkled in what could be a grin. She relaxes some, hand on door latch.

"Ma'am," says Stubby. "You trying to cripple yourself?" She just stares at him. "Man's work," he says. "Where's your man?"

"Inside," she says. Then, quick, "He's sick."

"Bad?" says Stubby.

"Was," she says. "Doctor that was here this morning thinks he'll be all right now. Only he's almighty weak. All wobbly. Sleeps most of the time."

"Sleeps," says Stubby, indignant. "When there's wood to be chopped."

"He's been almighty tired," she says, quick, defensive. "Even afore he was took sick. Wore out." She is rubbing cold hands together, trying to warm them. "He tried," she says, proud. "Only a while ago. Couldn't even get his pants on. Just fell flat on the floor."

Stubby looks down at her. "An' you ain't tired?" he says.

"I ain't got time to be tired," she says. "Not with all I got to do."

Stubby Pringle looks off past dark boles of trees at last row ridge top that hides valley and schoolhouse. "I reckon I could spare a bit of time," he says. "Likely they ain't much more'n started yet," he says. He looks again at the woman. He sees grey pinched face. He sees cold-shivering under bumpy jacket. "Ma'am," he says. "Get on in there an' warm your gizzard some. I'll just chop you a bit of wood."

ROAN STANDS WITH DROPPING reins, ground-tied, disgusted. It shakes head to send icicles tinkling from bit and bridle. Stopped in midst of epic run, wind-eating, mile-gobbling, iron-boned and dynamite-fueled, and for what? For silly chore of chopping.

Fifteen feet away Stubby Pringle chops wood. Moon is rising over last low ridgetop and its light, filtered through trees, shines on leaping blade. He is Stubby Pringle, moonstruck maverick of the Triple X, born with ax in hands, with strength of stroke in muscles, weaned on whetstone, fed on cordwood, raised to fell whole forests. He is ten feet tall and ax is enormous in moonlight and chips fly like stormflakes of snow and blade slices through branches thick as his arm, through logs thick as his thigh.

He leans ax against a stump and he spreads arms wide and he scoops up whole cords at a time and strides to door and kicks it open . . .

Both corners of front room by fireplace are piled full now, floor to ceiling, good wood, stout wood, seasoned wood, wood enough for a whole wicked winter week. Chore done and done right, Stubby looks around him. Fire is burning bright and well-fed, working on warmth. Man lies on big old bed along opposite wall, blanket over, eyes closed, face grey pale, snoring long and slow. Woman fusses with something at old wood-stove. Stubby steps to doorway to back room. He pulls aside hanging cloth. Faint in dimness inside he sees two low bunks and in one, under an old quilt, a curly-headed small girl and in other, under other old quilt, a boy who would be waist-high awake and standing. He sees them still and quiet, sleeping sound. "Cute little devils," he says.

* 18 *

He turns back and woman is coming toward him, cup of coffee in hand, strong and hot and steaming. Coffee the kind to warm the throat and gizzard of chore-doing hard-chopping cowhand on a cold, cold night. He takes the cup and raises it to his lips. Drains it in two gulps. "Thank you, ma'am," he says. "That was right kindly of you." He sets cup on table. "I got to be getting along," he says. He starts toward outer door.

He stops, hand on door latch. Something is missing in two-room shack. Trust Stubby Pringle to know what. "Where's your tree?" he says. "Kids got to have a Christmas tree."

He sees woman sink down on chair. He hears a sigh come from her. "I ain't had time to cut one," she says.

"I reckon not," says Stubby. "Man's job anyway," he

says. "I'll get it for you. Won't take a minute. Then I got to be going."

He strides out. He scoops up ax and strides off, upslope some where small pines climb. He stretches tall and his legs lengthen and he towers huge among trees swinging with ten-foot steps. He is Stubby Pringle, born an expert on Christmas trees, nursed on pine needles, weaned on pine cones, raised with an eye for size and shape and symmetry. There. A beauty. Perfect.

Grown for this and for nothing else. Ax blade slices keen and swift. Tree topples. He strides back with tree on shoulder. He rips leather whangs from his saddle and lashes two pieces of wood to tree bottom, crosswise, so tree can stand upright again.

Stubby Pringle strides into shack, carrying tree. He sets it up, center of front-room floor, and it stands straight, trim and straight, perky and proud and pointed. "There you are, ma'am," he says. "Get your things out an' start decorating. I got to be going." He moves toward outer door.

He stops in outer doorway. He hears a sigh behind him. "We got no things," she says. "I was figuring to buy some but sickness took the money."

Stubby Pringle looks off at last low ridgetop hiding valley and schoolhouse. "Reckon I still got a bit of time," he says. "They'll be whooping it mighty late." He turns back, closing door. He sheds hat and gloves and bandannas and jacket. He moves about checking everything in sparse front room. He asks for things and the woman jumps to get those few of them she has. He tells her what to do and she does. He does plenty himself. With this and with that magic wonders arrive. He is Stubby Pringle, born to poverty and hard work, weaned on nothing, fed on less, raised to make do with least

possible and make the most of that. Pinto beans strung
on thread brighten tree in firelight and lantern light
like strings of store-bought beads. Strips of one bandanna, cut with shears from sewing box, bob in bows
on branch ends like gay red flowers. Snippets of fleece
from jacket lining sprinkled over tree glisten like fresh
falls of snow. Miracles flow from strong blunt fingers
through bits of old paper bags and dabs of flour paste
into link chains and twisted small streamers and two
jaunty little hats and two smart little boats with sails.

"Got to finish it right," says Stubby Pringle. From
strong blunt fingers comes five-pointed star, triple
thickness to make it stiff, twisted bit of old wire to hold
it upright. He fastens this to topmost tip of topmost

bough. He wraps lone bandanna left around throat and jams battered hat on head and shrugs into now-skimpy-lined jacket. "A right nice little tree," he says. "All you got to do now is get out what you got for the kids and put it under. I really got to be going." He starts toward outer door.

He stops in open doorway. He hears the sigh behind him. He knows without looking around the woman has slumped into old rocking chair. "We ain't got anything for them," she says. "Only now this tree. Which I don't mean it isn't a fine grand tree. It's more'n we'd of had 'cept for you."

Stubby Pringle stands in open doorway looking out into cold clean moonlit night. Somehow he knows without turning head two tears are sliding down thin pinched cheeks. "You go on along," she says. "They're good young uns. They know how it is. They ain't expecting a thing."

Stubby Pringle stands in open doorway looking out at last ridgetop that hides valley and schoolhouse. "All the more reason," he says soft to himself. "All the more reason something should be there when they wake." He sighs too. "I'm a dong-bonging ding-busted dang-blatted fool," he says. "But I reckon I still got a mite more time. Likely they'll be sashaying around till it's most morning."

Stubby Pringle strides on out, leaving door open. He strides back, closing door with heel behind him. In one hand he has burlap bag wrapped around paper parcel. In other hand he has squarish chunk of good pinewood. He tosses bag-parcel into lap folds of woman's apron.

"Unwrap it," he says. "There's the makings for a right cute dress for the girl. Needle-and-threader like you can whip it up in no time. I'll just whittle me out a little something for the boy."

Moon is high in cold, cold sky. Frosty clouds drift up there with it. Tiny flakes of snow float through upper air.

Down below by a two-room shack droops a disgusted cowpony roan, ground-tied, drooping like statue snow-crusted. It is accepting the inescapable destiny of its kind which is to wait for its rider, to conserve deep-bottomed dynamite energy, to be ready to race to the last margin of motion when waiting is done.

Inside shack fire in fireplace cheerily gobbles wood, good wood, stout wood, seasoned wood, warming two rooms well. Man lies on bed, turned on side, curled up some, snoring slow and steady. Woman sits in rocking chair, sewing. Her head nods slow and drowsy and her eyelids sag weary but her fingers fly, stitch-stitch-stitch. A dress has shaped under her hands, small and flounced

and with little puff-sleeves, fine dress, fancy dress, dress for smiles and joy of living. She is sewing pink ribbon around collar and down front and into fluffy bow on back.

On a stool nearby sits Stubby Pringle, piece of good pinewood in one hand, knife in other hand, fine knife, splendid knife, all-around-accomplished knife, knife he always has with him, seven-bladed knife with four for cutting from little to big and corkscrew and can opener and screwdriver. Big cutting blade has done its work. Little cutting blade is in use now. He is Stubby Pringle, born with feel for knives in hand, weaned on emery wheel, fed on shavings, raised to whittle his way through the world. Tiny chips fly and shavings flutter. There in his hands, out of good pinewood, something is shaping. A horse. Yes. Flop-eared ewe-necked cat-hipped horse. Flop-eared head is high on ewe neck, stretched out, sniffing wind, snorting into distance. Cat hips are hunched forward, caught in crouch for forward leap. It is a horse fit to carry a waist-high boy to uttermost edge of eternity and back.

Stubby Pringle carves swift and sure. Little cutting blade makes final little cutting snitches. Yes. Tiny mottlings and markings make no mistaking. It is a strawberry roan. He closes knife and puts it in pocket. He looks up. Dress is finished in woman's lap. But woman's head has dropped down in exhaustion. She sits slumped deep in rocking chair and she too snores slow and steady.

Stubby Pringle stands up. He takes dress and puts it under tree, fine dress, fancy dress, dress waiting now for small girl to wake and wear it with smiles and joy of living. He sets wooden horse beside it, fine horse, proud horse, snorting-into-distance horse, cat hips crouched, waiting now for waist-high boy to wake and ride it around the world.

Quietly he piles wood on fire and banks ashes around to hold it for morning. Quietly he pulls on hat and wraps bandanna around and shrugs into skimpy-lined jacket.

He looks at old rocking chair and tired woman slumped in it. He strides to outer door and out, leaving door open. He strides back, closing door with heel behind. He carries other burlap bag wrapped around box of candy, of fine chocolates, fancy chocolates with variegated interiors. Gently he lays this in lap of woman. Gently he takes big old shawl from wall nail and lays this over her. He stands by big old bed and looks down at snoring man. "Poor devil," he says. "Ain't fair to forget him." He takes knife from pocket, fine knife, seven-bladed knife, and lays this on blanket on bed. He picks up gloves and blows out lantern and swift as sliding moon shadow he is gone.

HIGH, HIGH UP FROSTY clouds scuttle across face of moon. Wind whips through topmost tips of tall pines. What is it that hurtles like hurricane far down there on upslope of last low ridge, scattering drifts, smashing through brush, snorting defiance at distance?

It is flop-eared ewe-necked cat-hipped roan, iron boned
and dynamite fueled, ramming full gallop through the
dark of night. Firm in saddle is Stubby Pringle, spurs
ajingle, toes atingle, out on prowl, ready to howl, heading for dance at schoolhouse in the valley. He is ten feet
tall, great as a grizzly, and the roan is gigantic, with
wings, soaring upward in thirty-foot leaps. They top
out and roan rears high, pawing stars out of sky, and
drops down, cat hips hunched for fresh leap out and
down.

Hold it, Stubby. Hold hard on reins. Do you see what is happening out there in the valley?

Tiny lights that are schoolhouse windows are winking out. Tiny dark shapes moving about are horsemen riding off, are wagons pulling away.

MOON IS DROPPING DOWN the sky, haloed in frosty mist. Dark grey clouds dip and swoop around sweep of horizon. Cold winds weave rustling through ice-coated bushes and trees. What is that moving slow and lonesome up snow-covered mountainside? It is flop-eared

ewe-necked cat-hipped roan, just that, nothing more, small cowpony, worn and weary, taking its rider back to clammy bunk in cold line cabin. Slumped in saddle is Stubby Pringle, head down, shoulders sagged. He is just another of far-scattered poorly-paid patched-clothes cowhands who inhabit these parts. Just that. And something more. He is the biggest thing there is in the whole wide roster of the human race. He is a man who has given of himself, of what little he has and is, to bring smiles and joy of living to others along his way.

He jogs along, slump-sagged in saddle, thinking of none of this. He is thinking of dances undanced, of floorboard unstomped, of willing women left unwhirled.

He jogs along, half-asleep in saddle, and he is thinking now of bygone Christmas seasons and of a boy born to poverty and hard work and make-do poring in flicker of firelight over ragged old Christmas picture book. And suddenly he hears something. The tinkle of sleigh bells.

Sleigh bells?

Yes. I am telling this straight. He and roan are weaving through thick-clumped brush. Winds are sighing high overhead and on up the mountainside and lower down here they are whipping mists and snow flurries all around him. He can see nothing in mystic moving

dimness. But he can hear. The tinkle of sleigh bells, faint but clear, ghostly but unmistakable. And suddenly he sees something. Movement off to the left. Swift as wind, glimmers only through brush and mist and whirling snow, but unmistakable again. Antlered heads high, frosty breath streaming, bodies rushing swift and silent, floating in flash of movement past, seeming to leap in air alone needing no touch of ground beneath. Reindeer? Yes. Reindeer strong and silent and fleet out of some far frozen northland marked on no map. Reindeer swooping down and leaping past and rising again and away, strong and effortless and fleeting. And with them, hard on their heels, almost lost in swirling snow mist of their passing, vague and formless but there, something big and bulky with runners like sleigh and flash of white beard whipping in wind and crack of long whip snapping.

Startled roan has seen something too. It stands rigid, head up, staring left and forward. Stubby Pringle, body atingle, stares too. Out of dark of night ahead, mingled with moan of wind, comes long-drawn chuckle, deep deep chuckle, jolly and cheery and full of smiles and joy of living. And with it long-drawn words.

"We-e-e-l-l-l do-o-o-n-e . . . pa-a-a-art-ner!"

Stubby Pringle shakes his head. He brushes an icicle from his nose. "An' I didn't have a single drink," he says. "Only coffee an' can't count that. Reckon I'm getting soft in the head." But he is cowman through and through, cowman to the marrow. He can't ride on without stopping to check anything strange on his range. He swings down and leads off to the left. He fumbles in jacket pocket and finds a match. Strikes it. Holds it cupped and bends down. There they are. Unmistakable. Reindeer tracks.

Stubby Pringle stretches up tall. Stubby Pringle swings into saddle. Roan needs no slap of spurs to unleash strength in upward surge, up up up steep mountainside. It knows. There in saddle once more is Stubby Pringle, moonstruck maverick of the Triple X, all-around hard-proved hard-honed cowhand, ten feet tall, needing horse gigantic, with wings, iron-boned and dynamite-fueled, to take him home to little line cabin and some few winks of sleep before another day's hard work . . .

Stubby Pringle slips into cold clammy bunk. He wriggles vigorously to warm blanket under and blanket over.

"Was it worth all that riding?" comes voice of Old Jake Hanlon from other bunk on other wall.

"Why, sure," says Stubby. "I had me a right good time."

ALL RIGHT, NOW. Say anything you want. I know, you know, any dong-bonged ding-busted dang-blatted fool ought to know, that icicles breaking off branches can sound to drowsy ears something like sleigh bells. That blurry eyes half asleep can see strange things. That deer and elk make tracks like those of reindeer. That wind sighing and soughing and moaning and maundering down mountains and through piney treetops can sound like someone shaping words. But we could talk and talk and it would mean nothing to Stubby Pringle.

Stubby is wiser than we are. He knows, he will always know, who it was, plump and jolly and belly bouncing, that spoke to him that night out on wind-whipped winter-worn mountainside.

"We-e-e-l-l-l do-o-o-n-e . . . pa-a-a-art-ner!"